THE
DRAGON, GIANT
AND
MONSTER
TREASURY

selected by Caroline Royds
illustrated by Annabel Spenceley

G.P. Putnam's Sons   New York

First American edition, 1988
Copyright © 1988 by Kingfisher Books Ltd.
All rights reserved.,
Published simultaneously in Canada.
First published by Kingfisher Books Ltd., London.
Printed in Italy.
Library of Congress Cataloging-n-Publication Data
The Dragon, giant, and monster treasury.
Summary: A collection of tales from various
sources about the adventures of assorted
giants, monsters, and dragons.
1. Fairy tales. 2. Tales. [1. Fairy tales.
2. Folklore] I. Royds, Caroline.
II Spenceley, Annabel, ill.
PZ8.D7695 1988   398.2'1   88–4050
ISBN 0–399–21587–5
First impression

For permission to reproduce copyright
material, acknowledgement and thanks
are due to the following:

Bodley Head Ltd for *Assipattle and the
Giant Sea Serpent* from "Favourite Fairy
Tales Told in Scotland" by Virginia Haviland.
Puffin Books for *The Last of the Dragons* from
"Five of Us and Madeline" by E. Nesbit.
J. M. Dent and Sons Ltd for *Frightening the
Monster in Wizard's Hole* from "Nonstop
Nonsense" by Margaret Mahy.
Andre Deutsch Ltd for *King Calamy and
the Dragon's Egg* from "The Great Dragon
Competition and Other Stories" by John
Cunliffe. For *The Giant Who Threw Tantrums*
from "The Book of Giant Stories" by
David L. Harrison. Copyright © 1972 by
David L. Harrison. Reprinted by permission
of the author.

CONTENTS

THE
SELFISH
GIANT

by Oscar Wilde

Every afternoon, as they were coming from school, the children used to go and play in the Giant's garden.

It was a large lovely garden, with soft green grass. Here and there over the grass stood beautiful flowers like stars, and there were twelve peach trees that in the springtime broke out into delicate blossoms of pink and pearl, and in the autumn bore rich fruit. The birds sat on the trees and sang so sweetly that the children used to stop their games in order to listen to them. "How happy we are here!" they cried to each other.

One day the Giant came back. He had been to visit his friend, the Cornish ogre, and had stayed with him for seven years. After the seven years were over, he had said all that he had to say, for his conversation was limited, and he determined to return to his own castle. When he arrived he saw the children playing in the garden.

"What are you doing here?" he cried in a very gruff voice, and the children ran away.

"My own garden is my own garden," said the Giant. "Anyone can understand that, and I will allow nobody to play in it but myself." So he built a high wall all round it, and put up a notice-board.

9

He was a very selfish Giant.

The poor children had now nowhere to play. They tried to play on the road, but the road was very dusty and full of hard stones, and they did not like it. They used to wander round the high walls when their lessons were over and talk about the beautiful garden inside. "How happy we were there!" they said to each other.

Then the Spring came, and all over the country there were little blossoms and little birds. Only in the garden of the Selfish Giant it was still winter. The birds did not care to sing in it as there were no children, and the trees forgot to blossom. Once a beautiful flower put its head out from the grass, but when it saw the notice-board it was so sorry for the children that it slipped back into the ground again, and went off to sleep. The only people who were pleased were the Snow and the Frost. "Spring has forgotten this garden," they cried, "so we will live here all the year round." The Snow covered up the grass with her great white cloak, and the Frost painted all the trees silver. Then they invited the North Wind to stay with them, and he came. He was wrapped in furs, and he roared all day about the garden, and blew the chimney-pots down. "This is a delightful spot," he said. "We must ask the Hail on a visit." So the Hail came. Every day for three hours he rattled on the roof of the castle till he broke most of the slates, and then he ran round and round the garden as fast as he could go. He was dressed in grey, and his breath was like ice.

"I cannot understand why the Spring is so late in coming," said the Selfish Giant, as he sat at the window and looked out at his cold, white garden. "I hope there will be a change in the weather."

But the Spring never came, nor the Summer. The Autumn gave golden fruit to every garden, but to the Giant's garden she gave none. "He is too selfish," she said. So it was always winter there, and the North Wind and the Hail, and the Frost, and the Snow danced about through the trees.

One morning the Giant was lying awake in bed when he heard some lovely music. It sounded so sweet to his ears that he thought it must be the King's musicians passing by. It was really only a little linnet singing outside his window, but it was so long since he had heard a bird sing in his garden that it seemed to him to be the most beautiful music in the world. Then the Hail stopped dancing over his head, and the North Wind ceased roaring, and a delicious perfume came to him through the open casement. "I believe the Spring has come at last," said the Giant; and he jumped out of bed and looked out.

What did he see?

He saw a most wonderful sight. Through a little hole in the wall the children had crept in, and they were sitting in the branches of the trees. In every tree that he could see there was a little child. And the trees were so glad to have the children back again that they had covered themselves with blossoms, and were waving their arms gently above the children's heads. The birds were flying about and twittering with delight, and the flowers were looking up through the green grass and laughing. It was a lovely scene; only in one corner it was still winter. It was the farthest corner of the garden, and in it was standing a little boy. He was so small that he could not reach up to the branches of the tree, and he was wandering all round it, crying bitterly. The poor tree was still covered with frost and snow, and the North Wind was blowing and roaring above it. "Climb up! little boy," said the Tree, and it bent its branches down as low as it could; but the boy was too tiny.

And the Giant's heart melted as he looked out. "How selfish I have been!" he said. "Now I know why the Spring would not come here. I will put that poor little boy on the top of the tree, and then I will knock down the wall, and my garden shall be the children's playground for ever and ever." He was really very sorry for what he had done.

So he crept downstairs and opened the front door quite softly, and went out into the garden. But when the children saw him they were so

12

frightened that they all ran away, and the garden became winter again. Only the little boy did not run, for his eyes were so full of tears that he did not see the Giant coming. And the Giant stole up behind him and took him gently in his hand, and put him up into the tree. And the tree broke at once into blossom, and the birds came and sang on it, and the little boy stretched out his two arms and flung them round the Giant's neck, and kissed him. And the other children, when they saw that the Giant was not wicked any longer, came running back, and with them came the Spring. "It is your garden now, little children,"

said the Giant, and he took a great ax and knocked down the wall. And when the people were going to market at twelve o'clock they found the Giant playing with the children in the most beautiful garden they had ever seen.

All day long they played, and in the evening they came to the Giant to bid him good-bye.

"But where is your little companion?" he said, "the boy I put into the tree." The Giant loved him the best because he had kissed him.

"We don't know," answered the children. "He has gone away."

"You must tell him to be sure and come tomorrow," said the Giant. But the children said that they did not know where he lived and had never seen him before, and the Giant felt very sad.

Every afternoon, when school was over, the children came and played with the Giant. But the little boy whom the Giant loved was never seen again. The Giant was very kind to all the children, yet he longed for his first little friend, and often spoke of him. "How I would like to see him!" he used to say.

Years went by, and the Giant grew very old and feeble. He could not play about anymore, so he sat in a huge armchair, and watched the children at their games, and admired his garden. "I have many beautiful flowers," he said, "but the children are the most beautiful flowers of all."

One winter morning he looked out of his window as he was dressing. He did not hate the Winter now, for he knew that it was merely the Spring asleep, and that the flowers were resting.

Suddenly he rubbed his eyes in wonder and looked and looked. It certainly was a marvelous sight. In the farthest corner of the garden was a tree quite covered with lovely white blossoms. Its branches were golden, and silver fruit hung down from them, and underneath it stood the little boy he had loved.

14

Downstairs ran the Giant in great joy, and out into the garden. He hastened across the grass, and came near to the child. And when he came quite close his face grew red with anger, and he said, "Who hath dared to wound thee?" For on the palms of the child's hands were the prints of two nails, and the prints of two nails were on the little feet.

"Who hath dared to wound thee?" cried the Giant. "Tell me, that I may take my big sword and slay him."

"Nay," answered the child. "But these are the wounds of Love."

"Who art thou?" said the Giant, and a strange awe fell on him, and he knelt before the little child.

And the child smiled on the Giant, and said to him, "You let me play once in your garden; today you shall come with me to my garden, which is Paradise."

And when the children ran in that afternoon, they found the Giant lying dead under the tree, all covered with white blossoms.

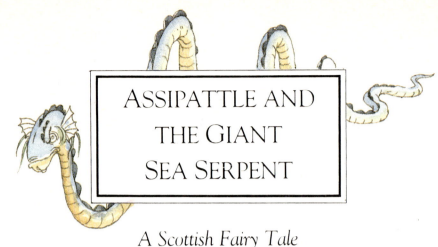

ASSIPATTLE AND THE GIANT SEA SERPENT

A Scottish Fairy Tale
retold by Virginia Haviland

LONG AGO in the north of Scotland there lived a well-to-do farmer. He and his good wife had seven sons and one daughter.

The youngest son was called Assipattle, because he liked to lie before the fire wallowing in the ashes. His older brothers laughed at him and treated him with cuffs and kicks. They made him sweep the floor, bring in peat for the fire, and do any other little job too low for them.

Assipattle would have been unhappy but for his sister, who loved him and was kind to him. She listened to his long stories about trolls and giants and encouraged him to tell more. His brothers, on the other hand, threw clods at him, and ordered him to stop his lying tales. What angered them most was that Assipattle himself was always the great hero in his tales.

One day something happened that made poor Assipattle very sad. A messenger came asking the farmer to send his pretty daughter to live in the King's house. She was to serve as maid to the beautiful Princess, who was the King's only child and much beloved.

Assipattle saw his sister go off, and he became silent and lonely.

After some time, another rider came by with the most terrible of tidings—that a giant sea serpent was drawing near the land. Hearing this, even the boldest hearts beat fast with fear.

True enough, a serpent came and turned his head toward the land. He opened his awful mouth and yawned horridly. And the noise of his jaws coming together again shook the earth and the sea. This he did to show that if he were not fed he would consume every living thing upon the land. He was well named the Master Sea Serpent—or the *Mester Stoorworm*—for he was the largest, the first, and the father of all the sea serpents.

Fear fell upon every heart, and there was weeping in the land. The King summoned his council and they sat together for three days. But they could find no way to turn the monster away.

17

At last, when the council was at its wits' end, the Queen appeared. She was a bold woman, and stepmother to the King's beloved daughter.

Sternly she spoke to the counselors: "You are all brave men and great warriors—when you have only men to face. But now you deal with a foe that laughs at your strength. You must take counsel with the sorcerer, who knows all things. It is not by sword and spear, but by the wisdom of sorcery that this monster can be overcome."

To this counsel the King and his men had to agree, although they disliked the sorcerer.

The sorcerer came in—a short and grisly man, looking like a goblin or bogle with his beard hanging down to his knees. He said that their question was a hard one, but he would give them counsel by sunrise.

Next day the sorcerer told the counselors that there was only one way to satisfy the sea serpent and to save the land. This was to feed the monster once a week with seven lovely lasses. "If this should not soon remove the monster," he said, "there will then be only one remedy—one so horrid that I must not mention it unless the first plan fails."

When people saw the serpent,
they cried: "Is there no other way
to save the land?"

Assipattle stared at the monster, and he was filled with rage and with pity. Suddenly he cried out: "Will no one fight the sea serpent and keep the lassies alive? I'm not afraid; I would fight the monster."

Everyone looked at Assipattle. "The poor bairn is mad," they said. His eldest brother gave him a kick and ordered him home to his ashes.

On their way home together, Assipattle persisted in saying that he would kill the monster. His brothers became so angry at what they thought was bragging that they pelted him with stones. Later, in the barn, they even tried to smother him with straw, but their father, coming by, saved him.

At supper, when their father objected to what the sons had done to their smaller brother, Assipattle answered: "You need not have come to my help. I could have fought them all. Aye, I could have beat every one of them had I wished."

They all laughed then and said: "Why did you not try?"

"Because I wanted to save my strength to fight the giant sea monster," said Assipattle.

Now over all the land there was weeping and wailing for the death of so many innocent lasses. If this went on, there would be no maidens left.

The council met again and called for the sorcerer. They demanded to know his second remedy.

The sorcerer raised his ugly head. "With cruel sorrow I say that the King's daughter herself must be given to the monster. Then only shall the monster leave our land."

The sorcerer pretended grief, but he knew it would please the Queen to be rid of the Princess.

A great silence filled the council chamber. At last the King arose—tall, grim and sorrowful. He said: "She is my only child. She is my dearest on earth. She should be my heir. Yet, if her death can save the land, let her die."

The counselors had to agree—but they did so in sorrow, for the Princess was beloved by everyone. When the head of the council, with sore heart, was about to pronounce the new edict, the King's own guard, who had stood by him in many battles, now rose and said: "I ask that, if then the monster has not gone away, the sorcerer himself shall become the monster's next meal." The counselors gave such a shout of approval to this that the sorcerer paled and seemed to shrink.

The King asked for a delay of three weeks, so that he might make a proclamation. He would offer his daughter to any champion who would drive away the monster.

Messengers now rode to all the neighboring kingdoms, to announce that whosoever would, by war or craft, remove the sea serpent from the land should have the Princess for his wife. With her would be given also the kingdom—to which she was heir—and the King's famous sword, Sickersnapper. That was the sword with which the great god Odin had fought his foes and driven them to the back side of the world. No man had any power against it.

Every young prince and warrior was stirred by the thought of a beautiful wife, a rich kingdom, and so great a sword. But, more than this, they were horrified by the edict that their beloved Princess was to be given to the monster unless someone drove it away.

Assipattle, hearing all this, sat among the ashes and said nothing.

Six-and-thirty champions rode to the King's palace, each one hoping to win the prize. But when they beheld the monster, lying out in the sea with his great mouth open, twelve of the number suddenly fell ill and were carried home. Twelve others were so terrified that they began to run away and never stopped till they reached their own lands. Only twelve stayed at the King's house, and these felt their hearts drop to their stomachs.

At the end of the three weeks, at evening before the great day when the Princess was to be sacrificed, the King gave a great supper. But it turned into a dreary feast; little was eaten, and less was said. There was no spirit of making fun, for everyone was thinking heavily of the morrow.

When all but the King and his faithful guard had gone to bed, the King opened the great seat on which he always sat. It was the high chair of state, and in it his most precious things were kept. He lifted out the great sword, Sickersnapper.

"Why take you out Sickersnapper?" asked the guard. "Your day for fighting is gone, my lord. Let Sickersnapper lie, my good lord. You are too old to wield her now."

"Wheest!" said the King in anger. "Or I'll try my sword on your body! Think you that I can see my only bairn devoured by a monster and not strike a blow for her? I tell you—and with my thumbs crossed on the edge of Sickersnapper I swear it—that I and this good sword both shall perish before my daughter die. And now, my trusty man, prepare my boat ready to sail, with her bow to sea. I will fight the serpent myself!"

21

At the farm that night the family made ready to set out on the morrow to see what would happen on the great day. All were to go but Assipattle, who must stay home to herd the geese.

As Assipattle lay in his corner that night, he found he could not sleep. His mind was filling with plans. And he heard his parents talking. His mother said: "I do not think I will go with you tomorrow. I am not able to go so far on my feet and I do not care to ride alone." His father replied, "You need not ride alone. I'll take you behind me, on Swift-go. None will go so fast as we."

Next Assipattle heard his mother say to his father: "For the last five years I have begged you to tell me how it is that, with you, Swift-go outruns any other horse in the land, while if anyone else rides him he hobbles along like an old nag."

"Indeed, Good wife," said the good man, "I will not keep the secret from you longer. It is that when I want Swift-go to stand, I give him a clap on the left shoulder. When I want him to ride like any other horse, I give him two claps on the right. But when I want him to fly fast, I blow through the windpipe of a goose. To be ready at any time, I always keep the pipe in the right-hand pocket of my coat. When Swift-go hears that, he goes swift as a storm of wind. So, now you know all. Keep your mind at peace."

Assipattle lay quiet as a mouse till he heard the old folk snoring. But then he did not rest long. He pulled the goose's windpipe out of his father's pocket, and slipped away fast to the stable. Swiftly he bridled Swift-go and led him out.

Knowing he was not held by his own master, Swift-go pranced and reared madly. But Assipattle remembered the secret and clapped his hand on Swift-go's left shoulder so that the horse stood still as a stone. Assipattle jumped on his back and clapped his right shoulder. And away they went.

22

As they were leaving, the horse gave a loud, loud neigh. This woke the farmer, who knew the cry of his horse. He saw Swift-go vanishing in the moonlight.

The farmer aroused his sons, and they all mounted and galloped after Swift-go, crying, "Thief!"

When Swift-go heard the farmer cry

"Hi, hi! ho!

Swift-go, whoa!"

he stopped for a moment. All would have been lost had not Assipattle pulled out the goose's windpipe. He blew through it with all his might. Swift-go heard this and went off like the wind, taking Assipattle swiftly beyond the others. The farmer and his sons had to return home.

As the day was dawning in the east, Assipattle saw the sea and lying in it the giant sea serpent he had come to slay. He could see the monster's tongue jagged like a fork, with which it could sweep whatever it wanted into its mouth. But Assipattle had a hero's heart beneath his tattered rags—he was not afraid. I must be careful and do by my wits what I cannot manage by my strength, he thought.

Assipattle tethered his horse to a tree and walked till he came to a wee cottage. He found an old woman fast asleep in bed. He did not disturb her, but took down an old pot which he did not think she would mind his using to save the Princess's life. In the pot he placed a live peat from the fire.

Now, with pot and burning peat, he went to the shore. Near the water's edge he saw the King's boat with sails set and prow turned toward the monster. In the boat sat the man whose duty it was to watch till the King came.

"A nippy cold morning," said Assipattle to the man.

"Aye, it is that," said the man. "I have sat here all night till my very bones are frozen."

23

"Why don't you come on shore for a run, to warm yourself?" said Assipattle.

"Because," said the man, "if the King's guard found me out of the boat, he would half-kill me."

"Wise enough," said Assipattle. "You like a cold skin better than a hot. But I must kindle a fire to roast a few mussels, for hunger's like to eat a hole in my stomach."

With that, Assipattle began to dig a hole in which to make a fire. In a moment he cried out: "My stars! Gold! Gold! As sure as I am the son of my mother, there's gold in this earth!"

When the man in the boat heard this, he jumped to shore and pushed Assipattle roughly aside. And while the man scraped in the earth, Assipattle seized his pot, loosened the boat-rope, jumped into the boat, and pushed out to sea.

The outwitted man discovered what had happened and began to roar. And there was greater anger when the King arrived, carrying his great sword, Sickersnapper, in hopes of saving his daughter.

With the sun now peeping over the hills, the King and his company could only stand on shore and watch.

Assipattle had hoisted the sail and was steering for the head of the monster. The creature lay before him like an exceedingly big and high mountain, while the eyes of the monster glowed and flamed like a fire.

The monster's length stretched half across the world and his tongue was hundreds and hundreds of miles long. When in anger, he could with his tongue sweep whole towns, trees, and hills into the sea. His terrible tongue was forked, and he used the prongs as a pair of tongs with which to seize his prey. With that fork he could crush the largest ship like an eggshell. He could crack the walls of the biggest castle like a nut, and suck every living thing out of the castle into his mouth. Still, Assipattle had no fear.

Assipattle sailed up to the side of the serpent's head. Then, taking down his sail, he lay quietly on his oars, thinking his own thoughts. When the sun struck the monster's eyes, it gave a hideous yawn—the first of seven that it yawned before its awful breakfast. Each time the monster yawned, a great tide of sea water rushed down its throat and came out again through its huge gills.

Assipattle rowed close to the monster's head, with his sails down. At the second yawn, he and the boat were sucked in by the inrushing tide. But the boat did not stay in the monster's mouth. The tide carried her on, down a black throat that yawned like a bottomless pit. It was not very dark for Assipattle, for the roof and sides of the tunnel were covered with a substance from the sea which gave a soft, silvery light in the creature's throat. On and on, down and down, went Assipattle. He steered his boat in midstream. As he went down, the water became more shallow, with part of it going out through the gills. The top of the tunnel began to get lower, till the boat's mast stuck its end in the roof, and her keel stuck on the bottom of the throat.

Assipattle now jumped out. Pot in hand, he waded and ran, and began to explore, till he came to the monster's enormous liver. He cut a hole in the liver, and placed in it his live peat. He blew and blew on the burning peat till he thought his lips would crack. At length the peat began to flame. The flame caught the oil of the liver, and in a minute there was a large, hot fire.

Assipattle ran back to the boat as fast as his feet could carry him. When the serpent felt the heat of the fire, he began to cough. There arose terrible floods. One of these caught the boat and flung it, with Assipattle, right out—high and dry on the shore.

The King and all the people drew back to a high hill, where they were safe from the floods sent out by the monster. The serpent was indeed a terrible sight. After the floods of water, there came from its mouth and nose great clouds of smoke black as pitch. As the fire grew within the monster, it flung out its awful tongue and waved it to and fro until its end reached up and struck the moon. When the tongue fell back on the earth, it was so sudden and violent a fall that it cut the earth and made a long length of sea where there had been dry land. That is the sea that now divides Denmark from Sweden and Norway.

Now the serpent drew in his long tongue, and his struggles and twisting were a terror to behold. The fiery pain made him fling up his head to the clouds. As his head fell back, the force of the fall knocked out a number of his teeth, and these teeth became the Orkney Islands. Again his head rose and fell, and he shed more of his teeth. These became the Shetland Islands. Finally the serpent coiled himself up into a great lump, and died. That lump became Iceland. And the fire that Assipattle kindled still burns in the mountains there.

And now everyone could plainly see that the monster was dead. The King took Assipattle in his arms and kissed him and blessed him and called him his son. He took off his own mantle and put it on Assipattle. And he girded on him the great sword, Sickersnapper. He took the Princess's hand and put it in Assipattle's hand, and he said that when the right time came the two should be married and Assipattle would rule over all the kingdom.

Assipattle mounted Swift-go and rode by the Princess's side. The whole company mounted their horses and returned with joy to the castle, where Assipattle's sister came running out to meet them.

Assipattle's sister told the King that the Queen and the sorcerer had fled on the two best horses in the stable. "They'll ride fast if I don't find them," said Assipattle. And with that, he went off like the wind on Swift-go, and soon caught up with the two. When the sorcerer saw Assipattle come so near, he said to the Queen: "It's only some boy. I'll cut off his head at once." But Assipattle drew Sickersnapper, and with

27

one dread thrust drove the sword through the sorcerer's heart. As for the Queen, she was brought back and made prisoner in a castle tower.

When Assipattle and the Princess were married there was a wedding feast that lasted nine weeks, as jolly as a feast in Yule. They became King and Queen and lived in joy and splendor. And, if not dead, they are yet alive.

28

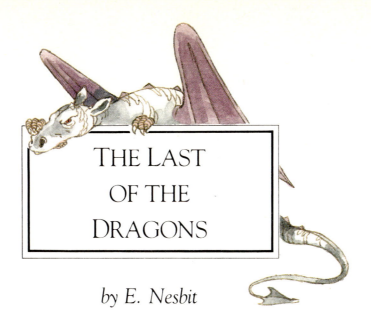

THE LAST OF THE DRAGONS

by E. Nesbit

OF COURSE you know that dragons were once as common as motor-omnibuses are now, and almost as dangerous. But as every well-brought-up prince was expected to kill a dragon, and rescue a princess, the dragons grew fewer and fewer, till it was often quite hard for a princess to find a dragon to be rescued from. And at last there were no more dragons in France and no more dragons in Germany, or Spain, or Italy, or Russia. There were some left in China, and are still, but they are cold and bronzy, and there were never any, of course, in America. But the last real live dragon left was in England, and of course that was a very long time ago, before what you call English History began. This dragon lived in Cornwall in the big caves amidst the rocks, and a very fine big dragon, quite seventy feet long from the tip of its fearful snout to the end of its terrible tail. It breathed fire and smoke, and rattled when it walked, because its scales were made of iron. Its wings were like half-umbrellas—or like bat's wings, only several thousand times bigger. Everyone was very frightened of it, and well they might be.

Now the King of Cornwall had one daughter, and when she was sixteen, of course she would have to go and face the dragon: such tales are always told in royal nurseries at twilight, so the Princess knew what she had to expect. The dragon would not eat her, of course—because the prince would come and rescue her. But the Princess could not help thinking it would be much pleasanter to have nothing to do with the dragon at all—not even to be rescued from him.

"All the princes I know are such very silly little boys," she told her father. "Why must I be rescued by a prince?"

"It's always done, my dear," said the King, taking his crown off and putting it on the grass, for they were alone in the garden, and even kings must unbend sometimes.

"Father, darling," said the Princess presently, when she had made a daisy chain and put it on the King's head, where the crown ought to have been. "Father, darling, couldn't we tie up one of the silly little princes for the dragon to look at—and then *I* could go and kill the dragon and rescue the Prince? I fence much better than any of the princes we know."

"What an unladylike idea!" said the King, and put his crown on again, for he saw the Prime Minister coming with a basket of newlaid Bills for him to sign. "Dismiss the thought, my child. I rescued your mother from a dragon, and you don't want to set yourself up above her, I should hope?"

"But this is the *last* dragon. It is different from all other dragons."

"How?" asked the King.

"Because he *is* the last," said the Princess, and went off to her fencing lessons, with which she took great pains. She took great pains with all her lessons—for she could not give up the idea of fighting the dragon. She took such pains that she became the strongest and boldest and most skillful and most sensible princess in Europe. She had always been the prettiest and nicest.

And the days and years went on, till at last the day came which was the day before the Princess was to be rescued from the dragon. The prince who was to do this deed of valor was a pale prince, with large eyes and a head full of mathematics and philosophy, but he had unfortunately neglected his fencing lessons. He was to stay the night at the palace, and there was a banquet.

After supper the Princess sent her pet parrot to the Prince with a note. It said:

"Please, Prince, come onto the terrace. I want to talk to you without anybody else hearing.— The Princess."

So, of course, he went—and he saw her gown of silver a long way off, shining among the shadows of the trees like water in starlight. And when he came quite close to her he said:

"Princess, at your service," and bent his cloth-of-gold-covered knee and put his hand on his cloth-of-gold-covered heart.

"Do you think," said the Princess earnestly, "that you will be able to kill the dragon?"

"I will kill the dragon," said the Prince firmly, "or perish in the attempt."

"It's no use your perishing," said the Princess.

"It's the least I can do," said the Prince.

"What I'm afraid of is that it'll be the most you can do," said the Princess.

"It's the only thing I can do," said he, "unless I kill the dragon."

"Why you should do anything for me is what I can't see," said she.

"But I want to," he said. "You must know that I love you better than anything in the world."

When he said that he looked so kind that the Princess began to like him a little.

"Look here," she said, "no one else will go out tomorrow. You know they tie me to a rock, and leave me—and then everybody scurries home and puts up the shutters and keeps them shut till you ride through the town in triumph shouting that you've killed the dragon, and I ride on the horse behind you weeping for joy."

"I've heard that that is how it is done," said he.

"Well, do you love me well enough to come very quickly and set me free—and we'll fight the dragon together?"

"It wouldn't be safe for you."

"Much safer for both of us for me to be free, with a sword in my hand, than tied up and helpless. *Do* agree."

He could refuse her nothing. So he agreed. And next day everything happened as she had said.

When he had cut the cords that tied her to the rock, they stood on the lonely mountainside looking at each other.

"It seems to me," said the Prince, "that this ceremony could have been arranged without the dragon."

"Yes," said the Princess, "but since it has been arranged with the dragon—"

32

"It seems such a pity to kill the dragon—the last in the world," said the Prince.

"Well, then, don't let's," said the Princess. "Let's tame it not to eat princesses but to eat out of their hands. They say everything can be tamed by kindness."

"Taming by kindness means giving them things to eat," said the Prince. "Have you got anything to eat?"

She hadn't, but the Prince owned that he had a few biscuits. "Breakfast was so very early," said he, "and I thought you might have felt faint after the fight."

"How clever," said the Princess, and they took a biscuit in each hand. And they looked here and they looked there, but never a dragon could they see.

"But here's its trail," said the Prince, and pointed to where the rock was scarred and scratched so as to make a track leading to the mouth of a dark cave. It was like cart-ruts in a Sussex road, mixed with the marks of sea-gulls' feet on the sea sand. "Look, that's where it's dragged its brass tail and planted its steel claws."

"Don't let's think how hard its tail and its claws are," said the Princess, "or I shall begin to be frightened—and I know you can't tame anything, even by kindness, if you're frightened of it. Come on. Now or never."

She caught the Prince's hand in hers and they ran along the path toward the dark mouth of the cave. But they did not run into it. It really was so very *dark*.

So they stood outside, and the Prince shouted: "What ho! Dragon there! What ho within!" And from the cave they heard an answering voice and great clattering and creaking. It sounded as though a rather large cotton-mill were stretching itself and waking up out of its sleep.

The Prince and the Princess trembled, but they stood firm.

"Dragon—I say, Dragon!" said the Princess. "Do come out and talk to us. We've brought you a present."

"Oh, yes—I know your presents," growled the dragon in a huge, rumbling voice. "One of those precious princesses, I suppose? And I've got to come out and fight for her. Well, I tell you straight, I'm not going to do it. A fair fight I wouldn't say no to—a fair fight and no favor—but one of these put-up fights where you've got to lose—no. So I tell you. If I wanted a princess I'd take her, in my own time—but I don't. What do you suppose I'd do with her, if I'd got her?"

"Eat her, wouldn't you?" said the Princess in a voice that trembled a little.

"Eat a fiddle-stick end," said the dragon very rudely. "I wouldn't touch the horrid thing."

The Princess's voice grew firmer.

"Do you like biscuits?" she asked.

"No," growled the dragon.

"Not the nice little expensive ones with sugar on the top?"

"*No*," growled the dragon.

"Then what *do* you like?" asked the Prince.

"You go away and don't bother me," growled the dragon, and they could hear it turn over, and the clang and clatter of its turning echoed in the cave like the sound of the steam-hammers in the Arsenal at Woolwich.

The Prince and Princess looked at each other. What *were* they to do? Of course it was no use going home and telling the King that the dragon didn't want princesses—because His Majesty was very old-fashioned and would never have believed that a new-fashioned dragon could ever be at all different from an old-fashioned dragon. They could not go into the cave and kill the dragon. Indeed, unless he attacked the Princess it did not seem fair to kill him at all.

"He must like something," whispered the Princess, and she called out in a voice as sweet as honey and sugarcane.

"Dragon—Dragon dear!"

"WHAT?" shouted the dragon. "Say that again!" and they could hear the dragon coming toward them through the darkness of the cave. The Princess shivered, and said in a very small voice:

"Dragon—Dragon dear!"

And then the dragon came out. The Prince drew his sword, and the Princess drew hers—the beautiful silver-handled one that the Prince had brought in his motorcar. But they did not attack; they moved slowly back as the dragon came out, all the vast scaly length of him, and lay along the rock—his great wings half-spread and his silvery sheen gleaming like diamonds in the sun. At last they could retreat no farther—the dark rock behind them stopped their way—and with their backs to the rock they stood swords in hand and waited.

The dragon drew nearer and nearer—and now they could see that he was not breathing fire and smoke as they had expected. He came crawling slowly toward them wriggling a little as a puppy does when it wants to play and isn't quite sure whether you're cross with it.

And then they saw that great tears were coursing down its brazen cheek.

"Whatever's the matter?" said the Prince.

"Nobody," sobbed the dragon, "ever called me 'dear' before!"

"Don't cry, dragon dear," said the Princess. "We'll call you 'dear' as often as you like. We want to tame you."

"I *am* tame," said the dragon—"that's just it. That's what nobody but you has ever found out. I'm so tame that I'd eat out of your hands."

"Eat what, dragon dear?" said the Princess. "Not biscuits?"

The dragon slowly shook its heavy head.

"Not biscuits?" said the Princess tenderly. "What, then, dragon dear?"

35

"Your kindness quite undragons me," it said. "No one has ever asked any of us what we like to eat—always offering us princesses, and then rescuing them—and never once, 'What'll you take to drink the King's health in?' Cruel hard I call it," and it wept again.

"But what would you like to drink our health in?" said the Prince. "We're going to be married today, aren't we, Princess?"

She said that she supposed so.

36

"What'll I take to drink your health in?" asked the dragon. "Ah, you're something like a gentleman, you are, sir. I don't mind if I do, sir. I'll be proud to drink your and your good lady's health in a tiddy drop of"—its voice faltered—"to think of you asking me so friendly like," it said. "Yes, sir, just a tiddy drop of gagagagagasoline—tha—that's what does a dragon good, sir—"

"I've lots in the car," said the Prince, and was off down the mountain like a flash. He was a good judge of character, and he knew that with this dragon the Princess would be safe.

"If I might make so bold," said the dragon, "while the gentleman's away—p'raps just to pass the time you'd be so kind as to call me Dear again, and if you'd shake claws with a poor old dragon that's never been anybody's enemy but his own—well, the last of the dragons'll be the proudest dragon there's ever been since the first of them."

It held out an enormous paw, and the great steel hooks that were its claws closed over the Princess's hand as softly as the claws of the Himalayan bear will close over the bit of bun you hand it through the bars at the zoo.

And so the Prince and Princess went back to the palace in triumph, the dragon following them like a pet dog. And all through the wedding festivities no one drank more earnestly to the happiness of the bride and bridegroom than the Princess's pet dragon—whom she had at once named Fido.

And when the happy pair were settled in their own kingdom, Fido came to them and begged to be allowed to make himself useful.

"There must be some little thing I can do," he said, rattling his wings and stretching his claws. "My wings and claws and so on ought to be turned to some account—to say nothing of my grateful heart."

37

So the Prince had a special saddle or howdah made for him—very long it was—like the tops of many streetcars fitted together. One hundred and fifty seats were fitted to this, and the dragon, whose greatest pleasure was now to give pleasure to others, delighted in taking parties of children to the seaside. It flew through the air quite easily with its hundred and fifty little passengers—and would lie on the sand patiently waiting till they were ready to return. The children were very fond of it and used to call it dear, a word which never failed to bring tears of affection and gratitude to its eyes. So it lived, useful and respected, till quite the other day—when someone happened to say, in his hearing, that dragons were out of date, now so much new machinery had come in. This so distressed him that he asked the King to change him into something less old-fashioned, and the kindly monarch at once changed him into a mechanical contrivance. The dragon, indeed, became the first airplane.

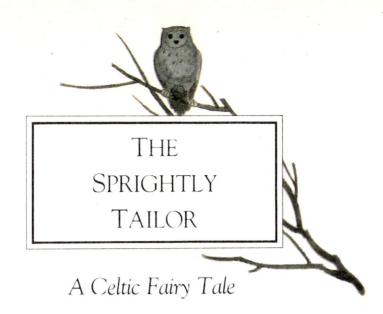

THE SPRIGHTLY TAILOR

A Celtic Fairy Tale

A SPRIGHTLY tailor was employed by the great Macdonald, in his castle at Saddell, in order to make the laird a pair of trews, used in olden time. And trews being the vest and breeches united in one piece, and ornamented with fringes, were very comfortable, and suitable to be worn in walking or dancing. And Macdonald had said to the tailor that if he would make the trews by night in the church, he would get a handsome reward. For it was thought that the old ruined church was haunted, and that fearsome things were to be seen there at night.

The tailor was well aware of this, but he was a sprightly man, and when the laird dared him to make the trews by night in the church, the tailor was not to be daunted, but took it in hand to gain the prize. So, when night came, away he went up the glen, about half a mile distance from the castle, till he came to the old church. Then he chose him a nice gravestone for a seat, and he lighted his candle and put on his thimble and set to work at the trews, plying his needle nimbly and thinking about the hire that the laird would have to give him.

For some time he got on pretty well, until he felt the floor all of a tremble under his feet, and looking about him, but keeping his fingers at work, he saw the appearance of a great human head rising up

41

through the stone pavement of the church. And when the head had risen above the surface, there came from it a great, great voice. And the voice said: "Do you see this great head of mine?"

"I see that, but I'll sew this!" replied the sprightly tailor, and he stitched away at the trews.

Then the head rose higher up through the pavement, until its neck appeared. And when its neck was shown, the thundering voice came again and said: "Do you see this great neck of mine?"

"I see that, but I'll sew this!" said the sprightly tailor, and he stitched away at his trews.

Then the head and neck rose higher still, until the great shoulders and chest were shown above the ground. And again the mighty voice thundered: "Do you see this great chest of mine?"

And again the sprightly tailor replied: "I see that, but I'll sew this!" and stitched away at his trews.

And still it kept rising through the pavement until it shook a great pair of arms in the tailor's face and said: "Do you see these great arms of mine?"

"I see those, but I'll sew this!" answered the tailor, and he stitched hard at his trews, for he knew that he had no time to lose.

The sprightly tailor was taking the long stitches when he saw it gradually rising and rising through the floor until it lifted out a great leg and, stamping with it upon the pavement, said in a roaring voice: "Do you see this great leg of mine?"

"Aye, aye: I see that, but I'll sew this!" cried the tailor, and his fingers flew with the needle, and he took such long stitches that he was just come to the end of the trews when it was taking up its other leg. But before it could pull it out of the pavement, the sprightly tailor had finished his task, and, blowing out his candle and springing from off his gravestone, he buckled up and ran out of the church with the trews under his arm. Then the fearsome thing gave a loud roar and stamped with both his feet upon the pavement, and out of the church he went after the sprightly tailor.

Down the glen they ran, faster than the stream when the flood rides it, but the tailor had got the start and a nimble pair of legs, and he did not choose to lose the laird's reward. And though the thing roared to him to stop, yet the sprightly tailor was not the man to be beholden to a monster. So he held his trews tight and let no darkness grow under

43

his feet, until he had reached Saddell Castle. He had no sooner got inside the gate and shut it than the apparition came up to it, and, enraged at losing his prize, struck the wall above the gate and left there the mark of his five great fingers. Ye may see them plainly to this day, if ye'll only peer close enough.

But the sprightly tailor gained his reward, for Macdonald paid him handsomely for the trews and never discovered that a few of the stitches were somewhat long.

BEAUTY AND THE BEAST

Fairy Tale

ONCE upon a time a rich merchant lived with his six sons and six daughters in a big house in the city. The boys were handsome and clever and the girls were pretty and clever, but the youngest child was the happiest and the prettiest and everyone called her "Beauty." Her sisters did not like this and were very jealous. They loved going to parties, trying on new clothes and visiting friends every day, and they laughed at Beauty who liked to stay at home reading or walking round her father's gardens.

Then suddenly the merchant's business failed and he lost all his money. He had to move with his children to a poky little house in a dark wood. No grand friends visited them now. There were no more parties and all the children had to work hard in the forest to earn money for food. Their clothes became tattered and they were often cold and hungry.

"It's all Father's fault," said the eldest sister.

"My hands are so rough," moaned the second.

"It's so dull here," declared the third.

"I hate the country," wailed the fourth.

"If only we had some new dresses," sighed the fifth.

"We could pick some flowers and make the cottage look pretty," said Beauty cheerfully, but her sisters went on grumbling.

After a while, the merchant heard that some of his money had been saved after all.

"I must go and see for myself," he declared.

"Take us with you," the children shouted, but he decided to go alone.

"Bring back dresses, perfume, jewelry, a carriage and horses," the other sisters cried, but Beauty said nothing.

"And what would you like, Beauty?" her father asked.

"Simply your safe return," she answered quietly.

"Stupid girl," scolded her eldest sister, but her father held up his hand. "Thank you, daughter, but there must be something you'd like, isn't there?"

Beauty hesitated. "Well, I love roses and as none grow here, perhaps you could bring back just one rose for me?"

The merchant set off on his horse in high spirits, but when he arrived in the city there was only disappointment for he found that all his money had been stolen. He had to set off for home with nothing except his poor old horse. As he rode along, a terrible snowstorm broke overhead. The merchant was cold and wet when he came to the edge of the forest, but he decided to try and reach home before nightfall. His horse stumbled through the deepening snow and at last stopped, for all the paths were now covered up. The merchant was in despair for it was growing dark and he was lost. Suddenly he noticed some very faint marks between the trees. Leading his horse carefully, he struggled along until all at once he found himself in a wide avenue of trees, all covered with flowers and fruit. The snow had vanished and instead he saw an enormous castle with wide open doors just in front of him. He led his horse through the doors and into a stable, then

46

entered the castle. How warm and comfortable it was! He peered into many rooms, all filled with magnificent furniture and treasure. The merchant was a little worried that there was no one about, for he didn't want to seem rude or inquisitive. At last he came to a small room where a fire was blazing and delicious food was laid upon the table.

"I'll just dry my clothes and warm myself," he said to himself. "This food must be ready for someone, so I'll wait for the master or his servants to come. He waited and waited until it was quite dark outside. By now he was very hungry so he ate a little food. Then he saw a comfortable bed in the next door room and he fell asleep.

The next morning, when the sun woke him up, he found a new set of clothes on a chair and a tray with fruit and hot chocolate nearby. Nobody came in and the castle was silent.

"Thank you, whoever you are, for your kindness," the merchant called as he went to saddle his horse. He passed some sweetly scented rosebushes and this made him remember his promise to Beauty. He had just picked one lovely rose when there was a terrible roar and a horrible Beast appeared. "I saved your life," the Beast shouted in a fearsome voice, "by giving you food and shelter. In return, you are stealing my precious roses. You are an ungrateful man, and for this you shall die."

The merchant threw himself on his knees. "I tried to thank you, kind sir," he stammered. "I didn't mean to upset anyone. I was going home empty-handed except for this rose." Then he poured out all his troubles to the Beast, and told him about his promise to Beauty. "Please spare me, at least until I've seen my family again."

The Beast glared at him, then said slowly, "I will forgive you on one condition. One of your daughters in exchange for you! She must come gladly and willingly and be brave enough to give her life for you. If

48

none of your daughters is willing, then *you* must return within three months. Swear to keep this promise."

The merchant promised at once, certain that he'd return himself, for it was impossible to give a daughter to this monster.

"You must go now," the Beast ordered. "But first fill a chest in the castle hall with anything you like, and it will be delivered to you. Remember your promise." With these words, the Beast crashed away through the bushes. The merchant quickly found a big chest which he filled with gold and jewels. "At least my children will have money now," he sighed, "even though I must leave them forever."

His horse was waiting at the castle gate with one perfect rose fastened to the saddle. Before long, the merchant reached home. All the children rushed out to greet him. Their father hugged them, but he looked sad as he handed the rose to Beauty.

"This is a most unhappy gift," he sighed, and told them of his adventures and his promise to the Beast.

"Stupid Beauty," screamed the other sisters. "Why didn't you ask for gold? Now Father must die for you and we will have nothing."

Beauty took her father's hand. "I will gladly offer myself to this Beast to prove my love for you."

"No, little sister," cried her brothers. "We will find this creature and kill him. Then you'll both be safe."

The merchant shook his head. "He is too powerful for you. Besides, I made a promise."

"Which I will keep," said Beauty quietly.

When the merchant went upstairs to rest, he found the chest full of treasure by his bed. "The Beast kept his word," he thought. "If he is so generous, perhaps he will spare Beauty's life."

Her brothers begged Beauty to change her mind, but she would not, so after three months she got ready for the journey through the forest. Her brothers were very sad, but her sisters were very happy with the gold from the chest and only pretended to be upset.

Beauty and her father set off on their old horse and soon reached the castle. The merchant led Beauty across the hall, which was blazing with lights, into a small room where a splendid feast awaited them. She was hungry after the ride, but her father was too miserable to eat. Suddenly there was a great crash, and the Beast stood before them. Beauty shook with fear at the sight of him, but she curtsied bravely, "Gggg . . . good evening, Beast."

The Beast was surprised.

"Were you forced to come here? Will you stay here without your father?"

"Yes, I will keep my promise," Beauty replied shakily.

"That pleases me," said the Beast, and then he turned to Beauty's father. "You must leave at dawn tomorrow. But first fill the boxes behind you and they will be sent to you."

He vanished. Beauty held her father's hand tightly before helping him to fill box after box with gold and jewels. Then, tired out, they

51

both fell asleep. In her dreams a fairy came to Beauty.

"You have a kind heart," she said. "Don't be sad when your father goes. And, most of all, do not think only of the outside of things."

Next morning, after breakfast, the merchant sadly begged Beauty to let him stay in her place. But Beauty kissed him and almost pushed him onto his horse. Then she turned away and quickly ran into the castle to hide her tears.

Inside, each room seemed more beautiful than the last. In one she found a picture of a handsome prince with a kind smile, and in another there was a locket with the same picture inside which Beauty hung round her neck. She saw no one all day, yet in the evening a delicious supper was ready for her beside a glowing fire in the little room.

As Beauty was eating, the Beast appeared. Was he going to kill her now? She held her breath, but he only said gruffly, "Good evening. What have you been doing since your father left?" At once Beauty told him about all the wonderful things she'd seen, and, as she talked, she forgot to be frightened.

"Will you be happy here?" the Beast asked after a while. "You can do whatever pleases you, at any time." There was a pause, then he added, "Do you think I'm very ugly?"

Beauty was terrified. What should she say? At last she replied gently, "I'm afraid I do."

The Beast sighed like the wind roaring.

"Well, enjoy your supper and I'll see you tomorrow," and he lumbered away.

That night the fairy visited Beauty again in her sleep. This time she was standing near the Prince's portrait. "Do not trust your eyes alone," she whispered before vanishing.

The next day Beauty explored the gardens; they were filled with flowers, fountains and singing birds, but there was not a gardener to be seen. At suppertime the Beast appeared again with a great roar and asked if she had enjoyed herself. Beauty chatted about the gardens and forgot to be frightened, until suddenly the Beast asked in his terrible voice, "Beauty, do you love me? Will you marry me?"

"Oh, Beast." She was very upset. "I'm afraid I don't love you." The Beast groaned like the roaring of the wind and turned away, head down and very miserable.

Each night Beauty dreamed the same dream, and each day she looked at the Prince's picture before reading, playing the piano, picking flowers, or trying on the wonderful dresses she found in the cupboards. "I'm just like my sisters," she laughed to herself.

Beauty now enjoyed talking to the Beast, but each night he would ask the same question, "Will you marry me?" and each night Beauty would answer, "I wish I could. I'm your friend but I do not love you." She was truly sad every time the Beast turned away with a deep sigh.

Beauty was not unhappy, but day after day the castle seemed so empty that she grew very lonely and longed to see her family once more. She knew now that the Beast was kind and gentle, even though he looked so fierce, so that night she begged him to grant her wish.

"I promise to come back, dear Beast."

"I can refuse you nothing," replied the Beast, "even if it kills me."

"I kept my promise before. I only want to see my father again. I would never hurt you or try to kill you." And Beauty began to weep.

"Then go," said the Beast, "and fill those boxes over there with anything you want. They will be sent to you." Then he held out a ring. "Take this ring and after two months, turn it round on your finger and say you are ready to come back. Remember, if you break your promise, I will die."

Beauty filled the boxes with presents, but in her dreams that night the Prince looked ill and weary, and the fairy shook her head sadly and said nothing. It was so strange that Beauty woke suddenly. The Beast's ring was on her finger but she heard her father's voice and knew she was at home. She rushed downstairs, kissed him and gave out all the lovely presents she'd packed.

While she was at home, Beauty did not once dream about the Prince. When the two months were up, her father begged her to stay. That night she dreamed she was in the castle gardens. She heard pitiful groans and saw the Beast lying under a tree, close to death. "The Beast will die tomorrow if you listen to your father," she heard the fairy whisper, and Beauty woke up, sad and frightened.

"I must go back," she told her family and she turned the ring, closed her eyes and said, "I wish to see the Beast again."

At once she was back in the castle, but it was all cold and dark. The flowers were drooping and the birds were silent. She ran along a path like the one in her dream and heard a feeble groan. There was the Beast lying deathly still.

"Oh, Beast, I've come back," Beauty cried, but the Beast did not move. She wept bitterly as she stroked his ugly head. "Please don't die, dear Beast. I can't bear to lose you. Your looks don't matter at all because I love you."

Instantly there was sweet music everywhere. She looked at the castle which was now bright with lights, then turned back to see the Prince of her dreams kneeling before her.

"Where is my poor Beast?" Beauty asked.

"Here, kneeling at your feet." The Prince smiled and took her hand. "A wicked fairy cast a spell on me and said I must stay like this—a monster—until a beautiful girl agreed to marry me because she loved me for myself. Beauty, you have broken that spell."

Now the fairy of Beauty's dream appeared. She clapped her hands and the Prince and Beauty found themselves back in the castle. In the hall, all their relatives and friends waited, gathered together by the fairy's magic. The Prince and Beauty were married that day. They forgave Beauty's unkind sisters and everybody lived happily together for very many years.

THE GIANT'S CLEVER WIFE

Traditional Irish Tale

FINN MCCOUL was a giant who lived in the north of Ireland long ago. He was building a bridge across the sea to Scotland that, to this day, is called The Giant's Causeway. Now Finn wanted a sight of his wife Oonagh whom he loved dearly, so he pulled up a whole fir tree, lopped off its roots and branches to make a walking stick, and he set off. Clean over the mountain tops he stepped and was soon at home at the top of Knockmany Hill.

His wife greeted him with a great kiss. "It's pleased I am to see you. Sit down and have the fine dinner I've ready for you." Finn ate twenty eggs, a whole oxen, fifty cabbages, and a great pile of delicious loaves, hot from the oven.

They were happy together, chatting over this and that, but Oonagh saw that Finn was troubled. "Why are you putting that great thumb in your mouth?" says she. She knew that Finn was touching a special tooth which could warn him of danger.

"It's himself is coming," says Finn. "It's Cucullin and doesn't he carry a thunderbolt with him that he flattened like a pancake with his fist?"

"Sure and you've beaten other giants, my fine husband," says Oonagh.

"Not one that shakes the entire country with one stamp of his foot. It's disgraced I'll be if I can't beat him," groaned Finn.

"Easy now. Go you and watch out over the mountains for this wee fellow," says Oonagh scornfully, "and by all the saints, I'll prepare a welcome for him. Indeed I will."

"You're a grand girl," declared Finn and out he went, leaving Oonagh to bake some very special loaves with iron griddles inside them. She was boiling a whole side of bacon when she heard a shout from Finn.

"He's coming and he's a terrible sight to see. It's a man-mountain he is. Glory be, I cannot fight him and him with that finger on him too." Everybody knew that all Cucullin's strength came from his forefinger and that without it he was just an ordinary man.

"Quiet, or you'll shame me," says Oonagh. "Now do as I tell you, my darling man, and put on this nightgown. And now this baby bonnet."

"Me! A baby. Never," screeched Finn.

"Stop fussing, man, or it's flattened you'll be! Now into the children's old cradle with you." Oonagh covered him with a quilt and pushed a baby's bottle into his mouth. "Lie there and trust me," Oonagh whispered. "He's coming."

She gave three long whistles, a sign that strangers are welcome, and, sure enough, there came a knock on the door like thunder.

"Welcome stranger. Come along in," called Oonagh, "and sad it is that my husband isn't at home to greet you."

"Would that be the great Finn McCoul?" And Cucullin himself walked in. "I'm sorry he isn't here for I'm told he is the strongest man in Ireland and I'd love to have the sight of him."

"Not just now you wouldn't," Oonagh said. "Some bastoon of a giant called Cucullin has been threatening him and Finn has rushed off to the Giant's Causeway to teach this boyo a lesson."

"I'm Cucullin," this giant roared, "and I'll be teaching him a lesson, I'm thinking."

Oonagh laughed. "Did you ever see Finn? You'd better hope that his temper has cooled before you meet him, for he's much bigger and stronger than you. Sit you down and take a rest. You'll need all your strength if it's Finn you're after fighting."

She turned to the oven and pulled out the bread. "Ah now, if the wind isn't blowing right through the house. While you're waiting, would you just turn the house around for me," Oonagh asked. "That's one of the little things Finn does when he's at home."

Cucullin pulled on his forefinger then went outside, picked up the house and turned it away from the wind. Finn trembled in the cradle. What was his good wife thinking of, he wondered.

Oonagh didn't show her surprise at Cucullin's strength. "Thank you," she said. "Dinner is almost ready but not a drop of water can I give you. Finn was going to find a new spring right behind those rocks, but he left in such a terrible temper that he forgot about it. Could you do that little thing for me?"

Cucullin heard water gurgling and knew his job was to crack open the mountain itself. He pulled his finger once, twice, nine times. Then he bent down and tore a huge hole right through the rocks. This hole is called Mumford's Glen even today.

Finn was terrified by Cucullin's strength but Oonagh calmly invited

the giant to sit down and eat. She brought the side of bacon, fifty cabbages, a pile of her special flat loaves with iron griddles inside, and a barrel of butter.

Cucullin picked up a loaf and took a huge bite.

"Cinders and ashes," he thundered. "Here's two of my finest teeth gone. What's in this bread, woman?"

"Why, nothing," Oonagh said in surprise. "It's the very bread I make for Finn and doesn't he eat twelve loaves just for his tea! You'll not be beating Finn McCoul, I'm thinking."

Cucullin seized another loaf. "Thundering thunderbolts, that's another two teeth gone." He was now in a terrible temper but Oonagh smiled sweetly. "It's glad I am that Finn's away for he'd kill you for sure."

The giant roared and stamped round the room. Finn let out a yell as Cucullin bumped into the cradle.

"Now see what you've done," Oonagh scolded. "If you can't eat a decent loaf of bread then at least keep quiet and don't go bothering Finn's fine little son." She winked at Finn. "Is it hungry you are, my pet?" and she gave him an extra special loaf without an iron griddle inside it.

"Flashes of fury," Cucullin growled, nursing his sore jaw as he watched Finn tear off chunks of bread and chew them with happy little noises.

"Is this truly Finn McCoul's son?"

"Indeed it is," Oonagh said proudly. "He only eats a few loaves each day but he is growing strong like his Daddy."

Cucullin was astonished. "That baby must have strong teeth if he can chew that terrible bread." This was Oonagh's chance! "Powerful strong, they are," she agreed. "You can feel them if you wish. You must put your forefinger right in, though, to feel the back ones. Open your mouth wide, little man." And Oonagh pushed Cucullin's finger right inside Finn's mouth.

Snip, snap. Finn bit off the finger. "You've tricked me," Cucullin bellowed as Finn jumped out of the cradle. He hit out with his

64

enormous fists but all his strength had gone with that finger. He turned and ran, down Knockmany Hill and away over the mountains.

Finn watched him go; then he and his clever wife enjoyed a grand dinner in peace. After that Finn went on building the Giant's Causeway across to Scotland but maybe he should have asked Oonagh's advice for it never was finished even to this day.

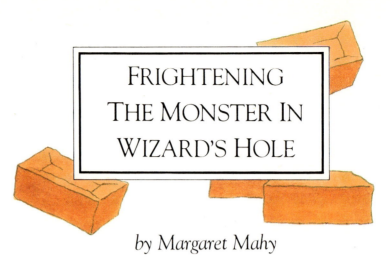

Frightening The Monster In Wizard's Hole

by Margaret Mahy

ONE DAY a truck load of bricks went over a bump and two bricks fell off into the middle of the road. They lay there like two newly laid oblong eggs, dropped by some unusual bird. A boy called Tom-Tom coming down the road stopped to look at them. He picked one up. It was a beautiful glowing orange-colored brick and it seemed as if it should be used for something special, but what can you do that's special with only one brick or even two.

"Hey Tom-Tom!" called his friend Sam Bucket coming up behind him. "What are you doing with that brick?"

"Just holding it," Tom-Tom said, "holding it and thinking . . ."

"Thinking what?"

". . . thinking that I'd take it and throw it really hard at . . ."

"At whom, Tom-Tom?"

"At the monster in Wizard's Hole."

Sam's eyes and mouth opened like early morning windows. "You'd be too scared."

"No I wouldn't. That's what I'm going to do now."

Tom-Tom set off down the road with his bright orange brick. Sam Bucket did not see why Tom-Tom should have all the glory and adventure. He grabbed the brick that was left in the middle of the road.

"Hang on Tom-Tom! I'm coming too."

"Okay!" said Tom-Tom grandly. "But don't forget it's my idea, so I'm going to throw first."

"Where're you two off to?" asked a farmer leaning over his gate.

"We're going to throw these bricks at the monster in Wizard's Hole," explained Tom-Tom.

"He's going to throw first and I'm going to throw next," cried Sam boastfully.

"You'd never dare!" cried the farmer.

"We're on our way now," they said together, strutting like bantam roosters along the sunny, dusty road.

"But how are you going to get the monster out of Wizard's Hole?" asked the farmer. "He hasn't looked out for years."

"I shall shout at him," declared Tom-Tom grandly. "I shall say, 'Come on, Monster, out you come!' and he'll have to come, my voice will be so commanding."

"I shall shout too," said Sam Bucket quickly. "'Come out, Monster,' I shall say. 'Come out and have bricks thrown at you.' My voice will be like a lion's roar. He'll have to come."

"Hang on a moment," said the farmer. "I've got a brick down here for holding my gate open. I'm coming too."

Off went Tom-Tom, Sam Bucket and the farmer, all holding bricks, all marching with a sense of purpose. They passed Mrs. Puddenytame's pumpkin Farm. Mrs. Puddenytame herself was out subduing the wild twining pumpkins.

"You lot look pleased with yourselves," she remarked as they went by.

"We are," said Tom-Tom, "because we're on our way to do great things. You see these bricks? We're on our way to throw them at the monster in Wizard's Hole."

reached the North Gate of the city, five weeks later. Their clothes were in tatters and the golden palanquin was spattered all over with mud.

King Calamy was told of their arrival. When he saw them, he said, "What in the world have you been doing all this time? Just look at you! What have you done with your horses? Where's the dragon's egg? Quick, show it to me."

Silently, Lord Pango lifted the lid of the casket. The king saw a mass of broken shell, and a dreadful smell made him bang the lid down again.

"Is—was—that it?" he said.

"Yes," said Lord Pango sadly, and told the king the whole story.

"Well, what are we going to do now?" said King Calamy.

"Send another expedition," said the Queen.

So he did. The same thing happened again, but this time they were attacked by another war-band, who smashed their palanquin to pieces and stole the casket.

"It's the palanquin and casket that attracts the brigands," said the Queen. "Send an expedition without these things."

So King Calamy sent an expedition with a plain wooden box to collect the egg in, but they were attacked and put to flight before they even reached the mountains. By now, all the wandering bands of knights knew that King Calamy was trying to get a dragon's egg for hatching, for rumor and gossip had carried the news all over the land. They were determined to stop him, because they knew that a new dragon would be a great danger to them. King Calamy sent out more expeditions, but every one of them was attacked as soon as it was well clear of the safety of the city walls. Soon, it became dangerous for any soldier or knight to leave the city at all, and King Calamy despaired of ever getting a dragon's egg.

Then the Queen had another idea.

"Why not offer a prize to anyone who can bring a dragon's egg safely to the city?"

"Why not?" said the King. "It's our last chance. Our enemies will attack the city soon, if we don't get a new dragon. Yes, we'll do it."

So the heralds proclaimed a prize of one thousand gold pieces for anyone who brought a good dragon's egg safely to the King. This gave David an idea in his turn—David, the boy who brought his father's eggs to market: brown hens' eggs; big duck eggs; still bigger goose eggs.

One day, instead of riding to town with his big baskets of eggs, he turned his horse toward the mountains. He carried simple provisions: bread and cheese, and a gourd of wine; and a small pan to cook eggs in. He soon met a roving band of knights, who were on the lookout for the king's expeditions.

"Who are you, and what is your business? What have you got in those baskets?" demanded their leader.

"I am David. My father has a small farm, with hens, ducks and geese. My baskets are full of eggs. I am on my way to the city beyond the mountains to sell my eggs, for I can get a better price there than in King Calamy's city. The people are poor there. All their money is spent in taxes to pay for fruitless expeditions."

The knight grinned at this, and said, "Go on your way, boy. We have no quarrel with honest traders, or with *duck* eggs."

And they let David go, unharmed. As he went on his way, he met many more bands of knights, and the same thing happened each time. When he reached the mountains, it was quieter, and he camped out many a night without seeing anyone. Then, he began to hunt for dragons' eggs. If he met anyone, he pretended simply to be traveling on toward the distant city, so that no one knew of his real quest. After many days of seeking, David was rewarded. He found a beautiful dragon's egg, nestling under some broad ferns. It was marked all over with fine crimson lines—the one sure sign of a dragon's egg, as he knew. He took some chalk dust from a pouch on his belt and rubbed it all over the egg, making it white. Now it looked just like a goose egg, even if it was a little bit larger. He lifted a number of goose eggs out of one of his baskets, made a space, and gently placed the dragon's egg in it. Then he covered it over with a good deep layer of goose eggs. He turned his horse round and headed back for home.

On the way back, David met many more bands of knights. Some looked suspiciously into his basket, but they all let him go on. It was quite obvious that he really was a seller of eggs, an innocent trader with no notions about dragons. David's worst moment was when he met a band of hungry knights, who were luckily honest and bought what they could easily have taken from him. They bought all his hen eggs, and all his duck eggs, and would have bought his goose eggs, too, but he said, "These eggs are for hatching, not eating, and so more costly. My father will beat me if I don't take them safely home; he hopes to hatch a great many geese for the Christmas fairs. Good, sir knights, please let me keep my goose eggs."

The knights laughed, and their leader said, "He shall keep his geese. Go on your way, boy; we'll not earn you a beating."

84

And so David came to the city gates at last, and went to the palace to tell King Calamy of his quest, and claim his reward.

85

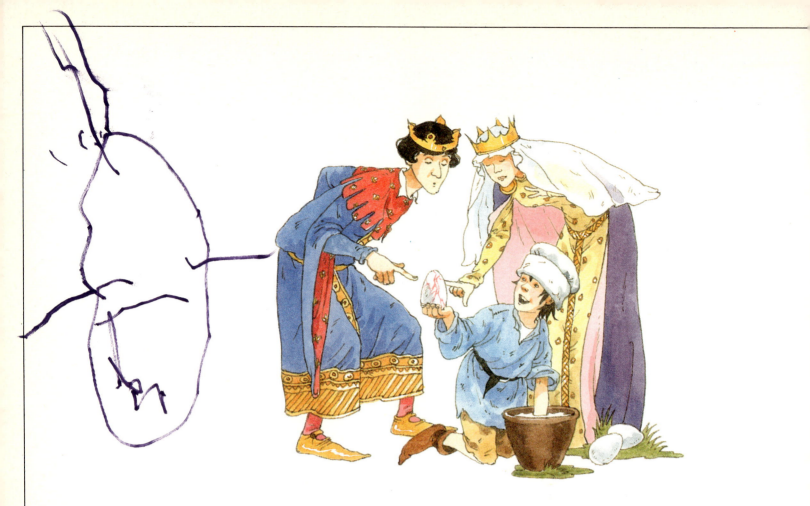

"Is it possible?" said King Calamy, looking in amazement at the basket of goose eggs. "Is it possible that a boy has succeeded where all my soldiers and brave knights have failed? Are you pulling my leg, boy? Come now, are you? It doesn't do to tease a king. I could have your head chopped off, just like that! You have dozens of eggs there."

"No, sire, it is true. I have brought you a dragon's egg. If you will send for a bowl of water, I will show you."

"Water? A bowl of water? The boy's crazy."

"Humor him," said the Queen. "Let's see what his game is."

Turning to a footman, she said, "Water. A bowl of water, at once."

The water was brought. David knelt before the king. He took his eggs from the basket, one by one. He washed each one carefully in the water and laid it on the grass. He could not guess himself, so good was the disguise—which was the dragon's egg; but he came at last to an egg that revealed a pattern of fine crimson lines when it was washed. He held it out to the king, in triumph.

"For you, your majesty. One dragon's egg. May I have my reward?"

"Indeed it is," whispered the King. "I have seen it just so, in my book of eggs. My boy, how did you do it, with the fields full of armed knights and brigands?"

"It was simple," said David. "I carry eggs to market every week. People are used to seeing me with baskets of eggs, so no one takes any notice when I pass by. When your knights march past with their glittering armor and bright flags, everyone notices, the word runs before them, and the enemy are on the lookout. No matter how your knights carried a dragon's egg, it would be found and destroyed. What better place to hide an egg than among a lot of other eggs?"

"No better place in all the world," laughed the King. "The boy has more brains than the rest of us put together. Give him the thousand gold pieces. He's earned them."

David returned home rich and famous. The egg was hatched, and a fine new dragon came out of it, and King Calamy's city was safe for another nine hundred years.

PREFACE
by Hermene D. Hartman

Martin Luther King, Jr. influenced my life in three stages; as a child, as a teen and as an adult. I was still in high school when Dr. King came to Chicago, but his activities had had an effect on my thinking even when I was in grammar school and he was in Birmingham, Alabama. We were studying civics in school, learning about the Declaration of Independence and the Constitution, and I couldn't understand the paradox between what we were learning and what I saw on television when I went home at night. I'll never forget the feeling I got when I saw dogs being released on demonstrators and water being forced on freedom marchers. In school I kept asking, "If we have natural rights, why are our people being bitten by dogs? If we are all created equal, why are firehoses being turned on our people?" And the teacher couldn't answer. At the time I thought he didn't see the paradox because he didn't know the answer. I didn't understand that he *couldn't* answer. It was very confusing and I asked the same questions over and over. The Constitution said very clearly that we all had equal rights but what I saw on television happening during the demonstrations showed it was not true. So I wondered if the Constitution was wrong. I kept asking, the way a little kid does, "Who's lying?" And at home I asked my parents, "If such things happen in the South, could they happen in Chicago? Do we need something like that here?" Dr. King had created a stirring, an awakening in me.

When Dr. King came to Chicago I wanted to march. My mother thought it would be dangerous. People probably would get hurt and some would go to jail. I didn't march. I wasn't afraid of the possible violence but I had to respect the feelings of my mother. Instead, I joined with the other Black students in my high school (there were eleven Blacks in a school of six hundred and twenty-five) and we carried signs in the halls between classes. We didn't miss any classes. We left a couple of them early to carry our signs, but we went everywhere we were supposed to be, and the rest of the time we walked up and down those halls with our signs.

Later my mother learned about Jesse Jackson's activities with Operation Breadbasket, which was the Chicago arm of Dr. King's Southern Christian Leadership Conference (SCLC), located on 47th Street on the South Side. Being a teenager, I was unwilling to give up school dances and such for something as seemingly insignificant as licking envelopes. Three years later, when Dr. King was killed, I went through a period of guilt about not having been involved. I thought, "I could have done something and I didn't."

I started going to the Saturday morning Breadbasket meetings that were held in the Parkway Ballroom on 45th Street. The meetings were attended by a cross-section of the community and among those were a little girl and her great grandmother whom I met there every week. Later I learned that the lady was Jesse's grandmother, Mrs. Matilda Burns (we call her Tibby) and Jesse's oldest daughter, Sandy.

The meetings were a form of community socializing, often accompanied by gospel-jazz music. But the main focus was the fiery sermons of Jesse Jackson and others.

These ministers talked differently than anyone I had ever heard. They generated such excitement. They preached about love, justice, and power, but what they said had more substance than just preaching. The Bible became a living story rather than an historical narrative. Jesus became an activist rather than a simple historical figure. These movement ministers told the audience how to bring about social change in a nonviolent way and provided a continuation of Dr. King's militant interpretation of Jesus.

I was very shy at the time, but I went up to Jesse after one of those meetings and volunteered to help. He introduced me to the Reverend Willie Barrow, who coordinated direct action activities and engaged at that time in a boycott of food chains unfair to blacks.

I went to the offices every day after school for an entire week. Too shy to ask what they wanted me to do, I just sat there. Finally I found Jesse and in frustration said, "I've been sitting here one week and I haven't done one thing. I came to help not sit." He replied, "Speak up. You have to let them know you're here." I started typing, doing clerical jobs and anything that needed to be done. Many of my friends wondered at me; not understanding that it was a commitment.

By this time I was attending Roosevelt University and studying political science. I combined the theory taught in school with the reality found at Breadbasket. David Wallace, Edgar Riddick, Gary Massoni, and James Bevel helped develop my concepts of social ethics and theology. I also learned much from other volunteers, people like Richard Thomas, Noah Robinson, Michael Knighten, St. Clair Booker, Lucille Conway Loman, the Reverend Calvin Morris, Larry Shaw, Cirilo McSween, Jack Finley, Leon Davis, Paul Walker, Al Johnson, George O'Hare, Jerry Bell, Al Robinson, Roberta Jackson, Dr. Alvin Pitcher and Jo Ella Stevenson. It was from these people I learned how to work and the work never stopped. I worked first with the Reverend Ed Riddick doing research, and then I started working with the Reverend Dave Wallace in the communications department. Here I met John Tweedle. He was the director-producer of a show called "Our People," on WTTW-TV. At the time he was the only Black television producer in town, and working with John and David I learned the basics of mass media communications.

I began to understand the need for developing positive Black images. We developed a trade fair and cultural "Black Expo" to promote Black businesses We began Black parades for Christmas and Easter with new symbols, such as, the Black Saint and the Black Lamb.

During those years we had what we called Workers Council, which met on Friday evenings. They were really leadership meetings, though no one called them that, and they went on for hours. Jesse lectured to about twenty of us about how to put our philosophy into action. He talked about strategies in boycotts, about how to get candidates elected, how to demonstrate effectively. He talked about issues. He talked about social justice. In essence, he presented a problem, an analysis and a solution. It balanced what I was doing in college. There we talked about the principles of the Federalist Papers, John Locke, Plato, Thomas Jefferson, and so on; then with Jesse we talked about Mayor Richard J. Daley and precinct captains. It was the theoretical contrasted with the practical; the history with the contemporary. All the while we were working to make change happen. My sense of values was maturing and I was learning how to take a project from its initial idea and work it through implementation to realization.

I learned that one person *could* do something. Working with those young militant ministers who wore jeans rather than three-piece success suits, I developed a sense that what I did mattered. I saw that ideas, concepts, and dreams could become realities if people worked on them in the right ways.

I remember the day Nelson Rockefeller, who was running for the presidential nomination, came to the South Side of Chicago and to our dinky little office to have his picture taken shaking hands with Jesse. This added a dimension to my understanding of power.

In a real sense, even as they have traveled different paths, Dr. King's lieutenants have had a ripple effect, shaping the persuasion of another generation. Dr. King's impact is beyond measure. We are still a long way from his dream of social justice and equal rights. We have much more work to do before bigotry and prejudice will be subjugated. But, he left us with a nonviolent but militant method. He made a lasting impression on people who were never in his presence.

He questioned his country's morality and sense of social justice and forced the country to reflect painfully. He changed Black America's self-concept.

He captivated people, influencing lives as they developed their own postures. He nurtured his students to become leaders in their own quest and even when they went their separate ways, they have persisted in his principles and teachings. He led leaders. He gave our people the power of dignity. He was a profound man in a profane world.

FOREWORD

Dr. Martin Luther King, Jr. *A Recollection*

By The Reverend Jesse L. Jackson

Everywhere he went and in everyone he touched there was change. He changed the image Americans had of Black heroes. Until this time Black heroes were limited to athletes and entertainers. As a young Baptist minister, Dr. King became a new kind of Black hero. He was a conqueror.

He changed me. As a young person growing up in Greenville, South Carolina, I was raised indirectly under his influence. At fourteen I became a student of the Civil Rights Movement. For the first time in this country the sense of Black revolt was so strong in the air that you could feel it. A non-violent revolution had begun. My direct involvement with this twentieth century prophet began the spring of 1965, when students and faculty of the seminary I attended responded to the crisis in Selma, Alabama. I soon found the man I came to call "Doc" was a wonderful teacher. He gave concise answers to my most complex questions. He made materialism seem infantile. He drove a Chevy. A station wagon has been my car. He taught me that the mission was more important than a vehicle. His wealth was in character, not things.

He changed the South. His journey began humbly and accidentally in December of 1955 in Montgomery, Alabama, when a tired seamstress, Mrs. Rosa Parks, refused to sit in her traditional place — the back of the bus. The twenty-six-year old minister was chosen by local Negro leaders to head what was to become a 383-day bus boycott that produced a Supreme Court decision making segregation illegal. It changed the course of history.

Dr. King applied the teaching of civil disobedience he had learned from the work of Mohandas Ghandi as a method to confront racism. His search for justice marked the decade of the sixties as a period of social chaos and consciousness raising. It was the beginning of an era Dr. King called "America's third revolution — the Negro Revolution." His organization, the Southern Christian Leadership Conference (SCLC), was formally organized in January 1957. He traveled throughout the South, with sit-ins, freedom rides, voter registration drives, marches, and selective buying campaigns to develop a New South. His Southern endeavors placed him in jail thirty times, usually with his partner, the Reverend Ralph Abernathy.

He changed the awareness of white clergymen. During his thirteenth jailing he wrote, "A Letter from Birmingham Jail," addressed to white clergymen, expressing the innermost feelings of Black Americans.

He changed the country's awareness of social injustice toward Black people. On August 28, 1963, he led the march on Washington. A quarter of a million Americans assembled in mass to support President John F. Kennedy's civil rights legislation. It was on this hot summer day Dr. King first said to the world, "I have a dream." King's theology was not about living to go to heaven or hell. He was an action minister expounding the social gospel. He was about the business of truth and love. He did not preach of death's redemption. He taught the transformation of a living situation. Because he raised questions, because he dared to care, because he accepted the challenge posed by Jesus, because he planted seeds, we bear his fruit to this day.

Because his organization, the Southern Christian Leadership Conference, led a voter's registration drive in Cleveland, the Honorable Carl Stokes was elected the first Black mayor of a major United States city in 1967. Because he raised issues of urban rot in Chicago in 1965, in 1983 the nation's second largest city has a Black mayor — Harold Washington.

He changed the North. In 1965, Dr. King decided it was time to come North to highlight that Northern racism was more concealed than in the South but still very much alive. He narrowed the choices to New York and Chicago, cities representing the nation's largest Black populations. SCLC staff people concluded New York's Harlem was too disorganized and fragmented. They chose Chicago, the hub of America's Black life. It was mecca for Black enterprise. Its political activity was unprecedented, and it had an effective political machine which could effect change. Its cultural life was rich. And Chicago had strong support from the religious community, Protestant and Roman Catholic, for civil rights efforts. The second largest city in the country had within it all the difficult problems faced by every other Northern city. As Andy Young, then executive director of SCLC said, "If Northern problems can be solved there they can be solved anywhere."

The pillars of Chicago's Black community — Edwin "Bill" Berry, Executive Director of the Urban League; Attorney Earl Dickerson; and the publisher, John H. Johnson, welcomed Dr. King. Albert Raby, convenor of a conglomerate of community groups, the Coordinating Council of Community Organizations (CCCO), extended the formal invitation to Dr. King.

So, he and his people chose the city discovered by a Black man — Jean Baptiste Pointe DuSable. The lakeside city with a beautiful skyline and a magnificent mile is where Dr. King's Northern Movement focused. The city was in for revolution.

During that period, I attended Chicago Theological Seminary, along with David M. Wallace and Gary Massoni. We three pioneered Chicago's Operation Breadbasket. In our last year of school, our lives were changed directly by Dr.

King's visit to Chicago. Dr. Alvin Pitcher, our ethics professor, helped us organize a minister's meeting held on Wednesday evenings, where we discussed social justice concepts. The Reverends Frank Sims, A.L. James, Clay Evans, Edmund Blaire, Stroy Freeman, the Reverends Claude and Addie Wyatt and Henry Hardy belonged to this group. As the ministers internalized these new ideas and impressions, their social attitudes and ministries changed. Not all accepted that. One minister became so disturbed by our thrust that he chased us out of the church with a loaded gun. And the Reverend Mr. Evans was severely penalized for his association with us. His new church building, Fellowship Baptist Church, stood unfinished for seven years because some politicians claimed he violated city building codes and his bank loan was held up.

It was in these conditions, in the heat of resistance, that the Chicago Chapter of Operation Breadbasket was born. We organized in 1966. We met on Saturday mornings. Our goal was to use the power of the Church to produce employment and business opportunities for Blacks. What began as an internship became a life's work. Neither David nor I returned to the seminary. On Christmas Day in 1971, Operation Breadbasket was transformed to Operation PUSH (People United to Save Humanity) and our first meeting was held in the Metropolitan Theatre, the "Met," just steps away from where the original Breadbasket offices were housed with CCCO on 47th Street, right off South Parkway. Since then, Saturday morning meetings have become a force that cannot be ignored. Local and national leaders have sought this platform to make important announcements and deliver major addresses.

When Dr. King assigned Dave and me to raise funds, we realized quickly that the more we could increase business and employment opportunities for the Black community, the more successful our fundraising efforts would be. Jobs, justice, and economic development became our campaign goals. Black businesses increased their targets from thousands to millions of dollars. Business reciprocity was significant to the Black community; it had a direct effect on the quality of life.

Such activity allowed me to be creative. I was promoted from Local Chapter Director to Northern Director, to National Director Operation Breadbasket

Dr. King's move to Chicago redefined the city. King was seen as a direct threat by the late Mayor Richard Daley, whose throne was shaken. The power political machine was troubled. Suddenly, orderly, obedient Negroes became socially chaotic. The city was becoming dismantled. For the first time in Daley's regime, where he ruled as Democratic Party king, another King trod. They locked into a heated power struggle. Marches, demonstrations, protests, rallies were daily occurences.

Marches into communities like Marquette Park and Gage Park became a part of Chicago's bloody history. Dr. King commented after he was hit in the head with a rock from the Gage Park open housing march that it had never been so bad in the Deep South. During the Gage Park demonstration, cars were overturned and burned, and policemen attacked from tree tops. Midwesterners were attacking a Nobel Peace prize winner on their front lawns. The urban jungle had exploded. Daley painted Dr. King as a "troublemaker." He tried to punish him, his workers and his supporters. Daley lost. He played short-range politics. Dr. King won. His strategy had long-range implications. He was planting seeds for social change. Plantation politics was dying. A new breed of politician was being conceived.

Ours is an extension of Martin's work. The natural evolution, the logical conclusion, of the civil rights revolution is in politics. Many other of Doc's people are there, including Andrew Young and Walter Fauntroy. In the fifties we raised the question of Blacks' right to vote; in the eighties we raise the question of the right to be President of the United States. Dr. King struggled for freedom;as a free people, we struggle for equality.

It is difficult to fit the man we called "Doc" into historical context. His life defies definition. He means so much to so many. He was Black America's first mass leader. He changed our minds about ourselves. He gave us psychological independence. He ended legal apartheid in America. Some have compared his life to Christ's, and it is true, life for Black Americans can be divided into two major eras: BK—Before King and AK—After King. He redefined the struggle, giving us a positive method for overcoming a negative situation, giving us successful means by which the least of us could fight.

This mild mannered man had a unique ability to articulate our groans. His message exceeded the race question; its essence dealt with love, power, and justice. He took Black America into the arena of global politics. As he interacted and related to power, he forced the world to view us with respect.

His legacy is he challenged a nation to succeed, to support its codes of ethics, to obey its own creed of conduct. He made America behave democratically.

He was martyred a young man, only 39, with many of his personal dreams yet to be realized. He didn't live to see his own four children grow to adolescence. He didn't live to see his disciples mature as leaders in their own disciplines. But his life was so full it could not be contained by a grave. He lives today in the changes he began. Martin did not make an annual contribution to the cause of freedom. He did not belong to the benefit banquet circuit. His life was devoted to liberation for his people. He made the ultimate sacrifice and we are the benefactors.

This is a better country today because of a Negro preacher's caring character.

JOHN TWEEDLE

July 5, 1936-December 8, 1981

Photography is an art. Photojournalism is art with generous amounts of intelligence, guts, sensitivity, dedication, compassion, mother wit, patience, stick-to-itiveness, technical skill, oomph, and much more mixed in. To understand John Tweedle, one has to realize that he had all these ingredients and more.

A photojournalist must be in tune with life; Tweedle was in tune with the spirit of life itself. He was a visual communicator who tapped the intrinsic values of life; he was a visual historian.

That old saying "never a dull moment"—that was true of Tweedle. He was like Santa Claus with no suit, just a camera, but always jolly. And he was tough, no one pushed him around. And no one ever went hungry around him; the food was always first class. He was flying above the dark clouds of life.

I first heard of John Tweedle at a photography seminar at the University of North Carolina at Chapel Hill. The speaker, Chuck Scott from the *Chicago Daily News,* talked about how great the city was and how great the paper.

"But," I asked, "are there any Blacks on the staff?"

There was a long pause, his head dropped, his voice changed, and Chuck told of being at the annual Chicago Press Photographers' Awards dinner a few months earlier.

Sitting at the head table was John Tweedle, who was to be honored as the first Black on a major Chicago newspaper. Just as the awards were being announced, a message was rushed up to the speaker.

"We have just received word, Dr. King was killed moments ago…"

Chuck told us how Tweedle dropped his head on the table and cried uncontrollably. And he told us how important John Tweedle was as a Black and as a visual communicator.

When I arrived in Chicago, Tweedle gave me a big brother welcome on the telephone and told me what he was going to do to me if I didn't start shooting great pictures, continuing the pace he had set. His call was a big surprise and a great challenge.

Before the week was over, I was covering a riot on Chicago's South Side from an unsafe position between the cops and the rioters. This big guy came over like a football player running interference, directing me to a safer location where I could still record the event. Tweedle became an instant coach-quarterback.

He was physically big and used it to his advantage in many situations, but it was balanced by that pleasant, childlike personality. He was caring.

Tweedle liked being around me; he was proud and happy for others to make it. He enjoyed being a team player and always played the big brother role. Black pride flowed through his veins. He gloried in being Black. He wanted others to know Blacks were working on major dailies. He got together a collection of my pictures and I became a guest on his TV show, my first Chicago TV appearance.

We laughed a lot together and shared many hours discussing personal issues, the world and Black responsibilities to society, and our foreparents; and many hours practicing our skills, attacking situations with the camera.

Tweedle was deeply aware of visual impact. His great eye, excellent skills, endless energy, and his ability to see and feel the whole scene enabled him to capture many angles of an event. He was a master of the technical. He enjoyed life's entire studio.

He always said that from events the mind retains images, visual images captured on film and then preserved not only in the photographic anthologies of the day but in the minds of millions who beheld them. And in this day of sophisticated journalism, where the written word is more critically prepared than ever before, and where live television takes us to events as they happen, it is still the frozen moment of photojournalism that is the mainstay of our memories.

Tweedle's camera was his passport to history. He truly lived the spirit of photojournalism. He understood lights and light, people and nature. He used his gift of sharing and giving something extra to life. He believed that where excellence is a daily habit, vision grows and his camera became an extension of his eye, heart and body.

His images are imprinted upon not only photographic paper but upon hearts and minds. He, too, had a dream: to share in book form what he saw and felt, with and for others—visual impressions of life. He knew that dreams come true and that seeds planted in rich soil produce good fruit. It's good to see this book, for those impressions will continue to be a part of us.

Tweedle and I always talked about winning a Pulitzer. It was December 8, 1981, following a meeting with my editors about my entry that I walked over to the photo desk, feeling a chill, knowing there was a touching story in the air. I was told that Tweedle had just died.

At first I felt lost, hurt, empty, but knowing Tweedle, he would have said, "Just keep on keeping on..."

I thought of his spirit of life and of living, his oomph for recording and sharing what he saw and felt and I felt a new challenge — like being handed a torch during a race. I thought of what a blessing it was to have worked with him. I remember during one of our last conversations, I'd said, "John, big brother, when I grow up, I'm gonna be like you."

And he just smiled...

JOHN H. WHITE—1982 Pulitzer Prize winner
Chicago Sun-Times Photographer

John Tweedle was a robust, jovial man. He never had to say, "smile," as he snapped the shutter. You looked into his round face and automatically responded that way. His human qualities represented the very best of living and loving.

John was a photographer's photographer. Many photographers could take pictures of the same event but people always wanted John's pictures. He saw things, moments, and events with a very special eye. John was the first Black photo-journalist hired by a major daily newspaper. He worked for the *Chicago Daily News* from 1964 to 1968 and rejoined the staff in 1974 where he remained until the paper ceased publication in 1978. Tweedle paved the way for many other people in the media, particularly photojournalists, two of whom have since won the Pulitzer Prize.

John's life was photography; rarely did you see him without his camera. He did not take pictures. He recorded moments. He documented time. He captured a spirit.

Tweedle was a master communicator. He earned degrees in Media Communications and advance degrees in Communications Science. He was a producer-director at Chicago's Public Television Station, WTTW-TV. Again, he was the first Black in Chicago to hold such a position.

When the Civil Rights Movement came to Chicago, John became its unofficial official visual recorder. On every major effort, at every event, he was there with his camera. He knew that the action was more than exciting, that there was history in the activity. He was aware and sensitive to the nuances of events as he delicately documented King's Chicago year.

Of his work he said, "If a photograph is to be effective it must immediately communicate a feeling or idea." John's wife, Dianne expressed his attitude this way, "John expressed many sides of life as he saw them. He followed as few rules as possible always believing that his love and instinct would guide him. He went for the picture that grabbed you in a vital spot and any vital spot would do. He believed a picture was graphically balanced when it moved you."

Perhaps the proper description of John is that he was a poetic photographer. Shooting just for fun one summer day, he caught former Mayor Michael Bilandic jogging on Chicago's lakefront. The photo appeared in *Newsweek*. Bilandic told John it was the best photo ever taken of him and asked if John would be his personal photographer. John did so, remaining at city hall until his untimely death.

This book reflects John Tweedle's vision and his unique sense of things happening about him. In this sense this photographic chronicle is as much about John as it is King. His photos speak to the sensitivity of shooting and the magic of the moment in the Movement. These are not staged, posed, studio pictures. They are recordings of a public figure working.

For years John and I had planned to prepare a book and an exhibit based on his photographs of Dr. King. We both sensed it was an important project. For five years, doing it was our New Year's resolution. Because we discussed the idea so often, I knew his favorite prints, all of which appear in the book. There are thousands of negatives; I have been through them hundreds of times. It has been difficult to choose which belonged. My final selections have been those photos which show Dr. King's many moods and represent the best quality from John's lens.

John Tweedle died of a sudden, massive coronary while at work in Chicago's City Hall, December 8, 1981. He was talking to his wife on the telephone about attending a Christmas party. He died with his cameras on.

In this book we have finally realized our New Year's resolution and through it the spirits of John Tweedle and Dr. Martin Luther King, Jr. live.

HERMENE D. HARTMAN

A LASTING IMPRESSION

A COLLECTION OF PHOTOGRAPHS
OF MARTIN LUTHER KING, JR.

To commemorate the silver anniversary of *Look* Magazine,
January 1962, the editors requested world figures to make pre-
dictions for the next quarter of a century.

"By 1987, I would expect the Christian era to
begin. Not because a balance of terror will have
paralyzed mankind, but because most of the world's
people will have realized that non-violence in the
nuclear age was life's last chance."

Dr. King appears at a press conference on welfare rights.
With *(left to right)* Bill Wiley, Executive Director of
National Welfare Rights Organization, unidentified woman,
and the Reverends Ralph Abernathy and Al Sampson, aides.

Dr. King and the press walk Hamlin Street.

The back yard.

When people heard he was there, they came in mass. His
move into the West Side slum attracted national attention.

The summer of '66 was besieged with demonstrations. Housing was a primary issue. People picketed in downtown Chicago, at the Real Estate Board Building.

Dr. King's protégés gathered in the rain for a "pray-in" on Chicago housing. Here *(left to right)* are Albert Raby, the Reverends Fred Shuttlesworth, Jesse Jackson and James Bevel.

Rallies were held in churches throughout the city
to bring an end to slums. He listened and he spoke.

SOLDIER FIELD RALLY

On Sunday, July 10, 1966, a "Freedom Rally" was held at Chicago's largest stadium—Soldier Field. The rally was sponsored by Dr. King's Southern Christian Leadership Conference (SCLC) and the Coordinating Council of Community Organizations (CCUO) headed by Albert Raby. CCUO consisted of over forty-four Chicago civil rights, religious, business, labor and neighborhood organizations. The two groups merged to become recognized as the Chicago Freedom Movement.

July 10th was a hot, blistering day. Junius Griffin, coordinator of the rally estimated the crowd at 65,000. They listened quietly as King spoke: "This day we must decide that our votes will decide who will be the mayor of Chicago."

He issued an emancipation proclamation to include thirty-five demands. After the rally, the huge crowd marched to City Hall and in the fashion of Martin Luther, founder of the German Evangelical Church and Protestant Reformation, posted a scroll on City Hall's main door, listing goals to make Chicago a racially open city. King's program included buying only from those firms that did not discriminate, keeping count of Black employees in business and public agencies, increasing the city's minimum hourly wage, demanding an open occupancy statement by public officials, seeking nondiscriminatory lending practices, and revoking city contracts with firms that lacked fair employment policies, desegregating Chicago public schools during the 1966–67 school year, creating a citizens' board to review police complaints, and replacing of absentee precinct campaigns in ghetto wards. A primary goal of the Chicago Freedom Movement was ending the city's housing discrimination. Dr. King said, "We must decide to fill up the jails of Chicago, if necessary, in order to end slums."

Stressing the importance of nonviolence, he said, "We must affirm that we will withdraw economic support from any company that will not provide on-the-job training and employ an adequate number of Negroes, Puerto Ricans, and other ethnic minorities in the higher paying jobs."

The summer of 1966 proved to be long and hot. The city exploded. Chicago became a changed city as a result of Dr. King's visit.

One of the community organizations participating in the
Soldier Field rally was The Woodlawn Organization.

Approaching the stage with Dr. King are *(left to right)* Ed Chandler, Executive Director, Church Federation of Chicago; and Edwin C. Berry, Executive Director of the Chicago Urban League.